☛ Two Scary Plays ☚

---

by
John Glass

"Finals With Felini"
and
"Give Me Something Good To Eat"

<u>Copyright information. Please read!</u>

☞ **About Student Plays** ☜

Student Plays consists of **John Glass, Jackie Jernigan,** and **Dominic Torres.** We are a group of playwrights and directors that have written scripts for elementary school through college. We are proud of the variety of ages that our scripts serve.

Student Plays has "creepy" plays, and we also have Latino-themed plays. These are scripts that focus on Latino youths and the Latino experience. Any school can perform a Latino-themed play: it just requires a general introduction and basic exposure to the Spanish language, something that most schools and students already have.

To contact *Student Plays* or to communicate with one of the playwrights, simply email us at john@studentplays.org.

☞ Finals with Felini ☜

A one-act play

Characters

DR FELINI   Female. College professor. 40s/ 50s. Eccentric. Angry.

MONA   Teens/early twenties.

AMBER   Teens/early twenties.

TY   Teens/early twenties.

MARTIN   Twenties.

The time is the present, the setting a college classroom. There are several chairs/desks in which the students are sitting and a typical table/desk for DR. FELINI, the professor. There are several tiny "straw puppets," or stick figures on the desk. There are also stacks of papers and books on the desk. It is the end of the semester and the class is taking a final exam.

The students are all dressed in typical college clothing. Dr. Felini is not dressed too conventionally. She should come off as a "bohemian professor." She can wear a scarf, have a nose piercing, or perhaps wear jewelry or something color-ful/unique that suggests an international or even a "gypsy" vibe.

At RISE: The class is busy taking a final exam. DR FELINI stands downstage, facing the audience, and opens the play with a brief monologue. Halfway through the monologue, MONA raises her hand with a question.

FELINI I've really learned to hate this class. Hell, I've really learned to hate this entire university. The administration. The dean. Ha. That woman's so pathetic and nosy.
    (Pause.)
 My department head, he's a blistering fool. These students aren't much better. Most of them, anyway. And yeah, I know . . . my time here is up. I'm ready to move on. But we've all got a boiling point. Right? And if these people want to push me over the edge, then they're in for a dark surprise.
    (Pause.)
Oh yeah. They're in for the unexpected.
    (Pause. She turns to face the class, notices MONA's raised hand.)
Yes, Mrs. Hamilton?

MONA Dr. Felini, are you sure we went over Woodrow Wilson's wife? Was she part of the review?

FELINI For the third time, *yes.* We talked about her last week. She should have been part of your notes.

MONA But I don't think some of us were here that day.

FELINI And just whose problem is that?? Hmm? Edith Bolling Galt was part of our classroom lectures, and thus part of our class! If you missed that day, then it's your responsibility to get the information.

MONA *(With a shrug.)* Okay . . .

> *(Beat. FELINI goes through the puppets and papers on her desk, staring off and speaking rhetorically. MONA sulks)*

FELINI Mrs. Galt . . . only one of the finest women to ever grace the White House! A woman that for a brief time called the shots for our country! After her doofus husband had a stroke.
> *(Looks back at MONA)*
You should feel ashamed for not knowing about her.

MONA But I missed that class! I told you!

TY I think I did too!

FELINI Enough, Mrs. Hamilton! Both of you! Finish your exam!

TY Sorry.

FELINI We've already gone over this. I'm not going to keep repeating myself. You are in college. Figure it out.

MONA *(Mumbling.)* It's just not fair.

FELINI Neither is inflation. Now, I've got work to do and so do you! Hop to it!
(She begins to exit, carrying papers.)
I'll just be right back here, down this hallway. Finish your exam.

(She exits. Pause.)

MONA This is so much crap.

TY She never told us that Woodrow Wilson's wife would be on the final!

AMBER Someone should go to the dean over this.

MARTIN I think she's already in trouble with the dean.

AMBER What??

MARTIN Didn't you hear all that drama earlier, before class? Out in the hallway, when she was on her phone? She was loud.

MONA I heard her. How unprofessional was *that?*

MARTIN I mean, I don't know for certain if that was who she was talking to. But something's going on. She's really been on edge.

TY Where did she go??

AMBER To hell, I hope. *(Pointing to FELINI'S desk.)* What the heck is Felini doing?? Why is she stacking all of that stuff up?

TY It's the end of the semester.

AMBER True. But it just seems weird. Her and her dumb little puppets. *(Pause.)* And what about those rumors?

TY Rumors over what?

AMBER About her dating one of the students.

MONA Who would date *her*?

MARTIN How do you know those rumors are true?

AMBER Well, I don't. But it's just weird . . .

MONA Agghh! I totally screwed this essay up. *(Balls up paper, stands and starts toward garbage can.)* How much time do we have left?

TY Uhh . . *(Checking watch.)* Thirty minutes.

> *(Enter Dr. FELINI, unseen by MONA as she throws the paper away.)*

MONA This is total crap! An hour for 4 essays! I hate political science!

FELINI You hate *what*??

MONA *(Turns to see FELINI)* Oh! Sorry! You know, I was just frustrated and—

FELINI Why are you walking around??

MONA I just had to throw a piece of paper in the garbage.

FELINI And why are you talking during a final exam??

MONA Well, uh, I was just saying how finals stress me out and—

FELINI *(Pointing to the hallway)* This way!!

MONA Huh?

FELINI This way!! You can take your exam in this room back here! Alone!

MONA Dr. Felini, I was just—

FELINI Now! The rules say no talking during an exam!

MONA I was just walking to the trash can!

FELINI And you were *talking!* The rules are written on the syllabus, in plain English. Now get your exam and pencil and follow me!

MONA I'm going, I'm going.

FELINI And please hurry! I'm very busy!

MONA Okay.

FELINI *(Escorting her to the door.)* Right this way.

> *(They exit. Pause. The others look at each other, dumbfounded.)*

AMBER Can you believe that??

TY She really *is* on edge.

MARTIN I told you. I think the department is fed up with her. With her crazy antics. It's all over social media!

AMBER Is it?

MARTIN Yeah.

TY Well, the proof that Bigfoot is *real* is all over social media and you don't see me believing it.

AMBER Guys, we need to stop! She's gonna give us *all* zeroes.

TY Tell me about it.

(Pause. They resume working. FELINI enters, muttering to herself, angry. She looks at AMBER.)

FELINI The nerve of *your* friend telling me we didn't go over Edith Bolling Galt. I hope your study habits are better than hers.

AMBER *(Nervously.)* Um . . . why are you looking at me?

FELINI Aren't you two sort of inseparable? You're always together.

AMBER Well—

FELINI Right? You two always sit together. You always snicker at the same time during my lectures.

AMBER Umm . . .

FELINI And here's something you can help me with: why do you two always come to my class late?

AMBER Well . . . sorry. We carpool.

FELINI Anyway, whatever. It doesn't matter! What matters is that you finish this exam. So, chop-chop.

AMBER I'm chopping.

(Beat. FELINI stares right at AMBER, coldly. She picks up one of the puppets, holds it as she speaks.)

FELINI You never really liked me, did you?

AMBER Umm . . what?

FELINI It's true. You never have liked me or this class. I see the way you roll your eyes. The way you and your little friend sometimes pass those notes during class.
(Sternly)
During my *lectures*.

AMBER *(Stammering.)*. I . . . I just—

FELINI Don't make excuses! You don't have to lie about it! Nothing on the syllabus says you have to *like* my teaching! Lots of people don't enjoy my classes. Only five of you signed up for this class and one of you didn't even show up for this final!
(She bristles as she paces in anger.)
You people are just like the administration. Just like Dr. Jones and those . . those . .

TY Those what?

FELINI Just never mind!! Stop talking! Finish your damn final! All of you!!

(She storms out, angrily. Pause. They are all floored.)

AMBER Dangggg.

MARTIN Is it just me or did Felini really flip out??

TY It's not just you. She *did* flip out.

AMBER This will be the last class I ever take with that woman.

TY Why is she walking back and forth so much?

MARTIN I think she's packing her stuff up. For the summer.

TY But shouldn't she be in here? What kind of college professor walks out of the class during a final exam?

AMBER The same kind that thinks it's important to memorize the wives of all the presidents.

MARTIN Tell me about it. *(Sarcastically)* Eleanor Roosevelt. Jackie Kennedy.

TY Don't forget about Dolly Madison and Lady Bird Johnson.

MARTIN Bunch of whiney liberals.

AMBER Hey. Watch it.

MARTIN Sorry.

TY *(Trying to concentrate.)* Guys, come on. Can't concentrate.

AMBER Yeah. Same here.

MARTIN Oh, wait. Is that her? *(Listening.)* Here she comes!

> *(FELINI enters quickly, talking on her cell phone.)*

FELINI Excuse me? Excuse me?? I did all of that! We had our end-of-the-year conference! Everything was properly checked out! Everything!
> *(Pause.)*

What? Okay, whatever. I have to go. I'm giving a final exam right now. I can't talk to you.
> *(Hangs up, paces in angry thought. She speaks*
> *rhetorically, while holding one of her puppets.)*

Do those idiots even know that I've taught all over Europe? Published over twenty academic articles? Taught for three years in Haiti? And the dean wants to lecture me on . . . *academic etiquette?* On *teaching methods?* Ughhh!
> *(She begins to exit, upset. She notices TY staring at*
> *her.)*

What are you looking at??

TY Uh . . .

FELINI Huh??

TY Sorry!

> *(She exits. Pause.)*

MARTIN What the hell's wrong with her?

TY Everything.

AMBER Guys? What was the name of Richard Nixon's wife? Her first name . . .?

TY Um. I don't cheat.

AMBER I just need her first name. You know. Nixon . . .?

TY I can't help you.

AMBER *(Struggling to remember.)* Agghhh. What was it?

> *(Pause. MARTIN looks at AMBER.)*

MARTIN Pat.

AMBER That's it! Right! Pat! Thank you!

(Returns to her writing. Pause. FELINI quietly enters, busy with a stack of papers. At first, she is not seen by AMBER.)

AMBER *(Still grateful.)* Yeah. Pat Nixon. I knew it was something like that.

FELINI Um, excuse me??

AMBER Oh . . !

FELINI You were just talking!

AMBER I was only talking out loud! To myself!

FELINI I beg your pardon?

AMBER I was just trying to talk out this answer. You know, to figure it out!

FELINI Silence! *(Pointing to the back room.)* Go back there! Now!

AMBER Dr. Felini, I was just trying to remember the name of—

FELINI Go! Now! You'll have to finish your exam back there, in a separate room. Alone!

AMBER But I—

FELINI Go! Unless you want a zero on the final. The rules are simple: no talking during tests. Now move it! Last chance!

AMBER *(Getting up quickly.)* Okay. I'm going. Jeez.

FELINI *(Escorting her out.)* Right this way. *(Looks back at the others.)* And you two remain quiet! No more of this nonsense!! No talking during the exam!

> *(They exit. TY and MARTIN are dumbfounded. Long pause before they begin to speak.)*

TY It's like we are in high school!

MARTIN No kidding! What the heck is she doing back there??

TY This is getting weirder by the minute.

MARTIN Weird? I'd say it's downright creepy.

> *(Beat. TY takes a long look at the hallway.)*

TY Look. I know we need to be quiet . . . but something is not right. I interned for Dr. Buckley last summer, and I know this classroom. I was in here all the time. *(Pointing to the back room.)* There *is* no room back there!

MARTIN What??

TY There is no room to take a test or *anything* back there! It's just a little hallway and a big storage closet.

MARTIN Then where are they??

TY I don't know! That's what I'm telling you. At first, I thought Dr. Felini just made that other girl sit in a chair or a desk. But how did she put *two* students back there??

MARTIN Are you sure there's no door?? Or maybe a—

TY There's nothing! I worked in this room almost all of last summer. I would have seen it!

MARTIN What . . . what do we do?

>   (*Pause. TY gets up, slowly walks towards the hall way*)

TY I'm going to get Felini in here.

MARTIN Don't do that!! Come on, she's already flipped out! Isn't it obvious?

TY How come we can't even hear them?

MARTIN Well, they have to be totally quiet. You heard what Felini said!

TY No. Something is happening . . . . (*Calls out.*) Dr. Felini? Hello?

MARTIN What are you doing??

TY Dr. Felini?

MARTIN Stop! You can't go back there!

TY Guys . . .?

(*Pause. Silence. They look at each other.*)

TY See? Something's not right.

MARTIN Where the hell is she?

TY I'm gonna find out. (*Begins to exit.*)

MARTIN No! Dude, she's gonna give you an F!

TY Dr. Felini? Guys . . ? (*Off*) Hello . . ?

(*Long pause. MARTIN writes a little more, then puts his pencil down. He quickly gets up and goes to a cabinet or closet, produces two duffel handbags or suitcases. Enter FELINI, slowly.*)

FELINI Hello!

MARTIN Well? All done?

FELINI Yes! All done!

MARTIN Yeah! That's my girl!

(They come together and kiss.)

MARTIN How was it?

FELINI Nothing to it! There never is!

MARTIN Nice. *(Peering back at the hallway)* Um. Did you . . . did you do that *thing?*

FELINI Yes. You know I did. I told you I was.

MARTIN Okay. Uh, where did you put the . . . bodies?

FELINI *(Kissing him again.)* Oh, never mind that! Don't worry! Everything is out of sight.

MARTIN Okay.

FELINI It's all done.

MARTIN Okay.

FELINI Now come on. We've got a plane to catch.

MARTIN Right, I know. Okay, well, here is your bag.

FELINI Great.

MARTIN *(Looking at his phone.)* I've got us all checked in.

FELINI Good, good. The tickets are in your name, right?

MARTIN Yes.

FELINI *(Looks around the room, assessing everything.)* Let's see . . . I've got my personal things. I've got the books I want.

MARTIN Nothing is here that can be traced? No addresses? Phone numbers?

FELINI No. Nothing. Took care of all that. All done.
    (Sees her puppets and collects them.)
Oh. Can't forget these!

MARTIN Yeah, your little friends there.

FELINI Yep.

MARTIN Okay, let's get out of here. The car is just out back, in the first lot. Very close.

    (Beat. She comes to a stop and looks at him.)

MARTIN Um . . . you ready?

FELINI Yes. But I just want to show you one thing. Come . . . *(Taking his hand.)*

MARTIN Heidi, we've got to go! The other exams will be ending soon!

FELINI I just want to show you one tiny thing. Really quickly. You're gonna love it!

MARTIN What is it?

FELINI Just come! *(Tugging him towards the hallway.)* It'll be very quick. I promise!

MARTIN *(Coming to a stop.)* But . . what is it?

FELINI You trust me. Right?

MARTIN Yes.

FELINI Are you sure?

MARTIN Yes.

> *(They quickly kiss. She coaxes him towards the exit again.)*

FELINI So, come. It won't take but a minute. You are going to love this!

MARTIN Okay.

FELINI That's my man.

MARTIN That's me.

(They exit. Long pause. Complete silence.)

MARTIN *(Offstage.)* What are you . . . ? What? HEIDI! No . . . not *that!!* NO!!

(Pause. MARTIN screams again. Pause. He screams once more. Silence. End of play.)

☛ GIVE ME SOMETHING GOOD TO EAT ☚

--

A one-act play

CHARACTERS

ANN   Late twenties. Therapist.
                 Compassionate. Strong convictions.

HOWARD   Twenties. College student.
                 Kind, deferring. Troubled.

MEREDITH   Twenties. College student. Kind
                 but very proud.

The time is the present, the place is Mason, Ohio, a suburb of Cincinnati. It is Halloween night.

The play takes place in the living room of Meredith's house. A basic setup of sofa, chairs, and coffee table. There is a table near the door, and one large bowl of candy. Several light-sticks are lying about, and one large bag of candy is on the floor near the door. There are a few Halloween decorations, such as orange streamers, a hanging paper skeleton, pumpkins.

HOWARD and MEREDITH are dressed in everyday clothing. ANN is wearing a witch's hat/costume. There is a
band-aid on the forehead of MEREDITH.

The unwrapping of the candy throughout the play should be
conspicuously loud. On page 40, HOWARD begins to eat
candy from the bowl and this should be very open and obvious.

At RISE: *As the lights go up, HOWARD and ANN are standing and talking. ANN is toying with her cell phone. The sound of a loud witch cackle is heard. After a few seconds it fades.*

HOWARD Isn't that a little much, Ann?

ANN Much? It's Halloween!

HOWARD Ugghh . . . It's *been* Halloween around here.

ANN Oh, come on. I love it. *(Pause. She turns the sound off and the laughter stops. She skims through her phone.)* Actually, I hope that I didn't wake Meredith up with that.

HOWARD I doubt it. She passed out hard after her last class.

ANN How late was she up last night? Till three?

HOWARD Three-thirty. I actually heard her car when she pulled in.

ANN That poor girl . . . *(Still occupied with phone.)* I have a huge Halloween play list. I'll just play these later. *(Beat.)* You got the diet Coke, right?

HOWARD In the kitchen.

ANN Okay. And you brought in those cheese fries, too?

HOWARD Yes.

ANN Good. Cold cheese fries. She loves those things.
*(Pause. She runs her fingers through the bowl of
candy and picks some pieces out.)*
Hey, thanks again for everything. For being here. I don't
know who else Meredith would have turned to.

HOWARD *(Sitting down.)* You've done more than your
share as well.

ANN Well, it's my job. But I guess I've also become at-
tached to this family.

HOWARD Yeah.

ANN *(Eating candy.)* I love these things. Yummmm.

HOWARD I don't know. I still say that . . . they made a
mistake.

ANN Huh?

HOWARD They shouldn't have released her so soon.

ANN Come on. Mrs. Allen will be fine.

HOWARD She was only in there overnight! And how are
you going to tell Meredith that she's already out?

ANN She's not worried. They've been through this before. Mrs. Allen's had her medication and—

HOWARD *Medication.* That means nothing.

ANN It means *something.* It helps. And Mrs. Allen isn't the witch some people make her out to be.

HOWARD Then how do you explain the bump on Meredith's head?

ANN She fell. She told us.

(Pause. HOWARD sits in thought, still troubled.)

HOWARD What about the fire? Mrs. Allen had all the burners on the stove going at once and she *forgot??* Do you really buy that?

ANN She's almost seventy years old. You know how forgetful she can be.

HOWARD That's what she wants us to think.

ANN Oh, please . . .

HOWARD The point is that something just feels wrong. Meredith is a very proud person. She wants people to think they have a normal family. But she's holding something back. I can tell.

ANN Give me a break . . .

(Doorbell rings.)

HOWARD Candy time.

ANN Yep! There's some more of the kiddos! *(Opens door, passes out candy.)* Happy Halloween! Look at you guys!! Ohhhhh! Here we go. Two for you, and two for you! Okay?? Bye! *(Closes door.)*

HOWARD You really are into this, aren't you?

ANN I can recall every Halloween since high school!

HOWARD Sheesh.

(Beat. ANN sees the extra bag of candy on the floor.)

ANN What is this bag? Extra candy?

HOWARD Yep. When I was out in the garage getting more paper towels for Meredith I saw it. So I just brought it inside.

ANN Okay.

HOWARD I put it out for the trick or treaters. It has all the chocolates and the good stuff. The other bowl has just peppermints and boring candy.

ANN Excellent. Good candy is a must! *(Throws a piece of candy at him)*

HOWARD Hey!

ANN I'm gonna put a hex on you!

HOWARD With all that's going on over here, I feel like I've *been* in a hex.

ANN Amen. But come on, it's Halloween. It's time to relax, right? I know I've been working hard. But you're always over here, helping out.

HOWARD Yeah. Well, I care about this family. We're neighbors.

ANN Sure you don't want to come with us tonight? It's in this old warehouse loft.

HOWARD Yes, I know about it. But no, I've gotta get up early. Eight o'clock class.

ANN Okay. I haven't gone to a haunted house in years. Kinda excited.

HOWARD I doubt that Meredith will want to go either.

ANN I know. But I had to invite her. Tried to get her out of the house for a few hours. You guys can bring over some food for her tomorrow?

HOWARD Yep. My mom is making her egg salad.

ANN Good. They'll be finished repairing the kitchen by Friday. Then she can use the stove.

HOWARD Okay.

> *(Beat.)*

HOWARD Ann . . .?

ANN What?

HOWARD There's just something . . . really weird here.

ANN Please! No more concerns!

HOWARD Something about the way Meredith looked at me this morning. When we left the campus.

ANN Ehhhh . . .

HOWARD And a few days ago she texted me that she didn't want to be here anymore. She was scared of something.

ANN Stop. She's not scared.

HOWARD She *is* scared.

ANN Oh, geez. She's just worried about her mother. That's all.

(Doorbell rings. She goes to the door.)

HOWARD I'm telling you. There's something there . . .

ANN It's fine! *(Opens door.)* Hello! Oh, you guys are so cute! Look at you! Okay, here you go . . . one for each of you. Okay!! Super! Happy Halloween! Ha ha! Bye! *(Closes door.)*

HOWARD How do you explain the fact that she called the facility on her own mom?

ANN Howard, Meredith just overreacted. She's just weary. Exhausted. We went over all of this.

HOWARD I just don't think Mrs. Allen is fit to be on her own. She almost burned this house down!

ANN It was an accident.

HOWARD It's ridiculous that they released her.

ANN She was properly assessed; she'll be fine. She'll stay at her sister's for a while. The time apart will be good for them.

HOWARD A lot of people are *assessed* and given a release, aren't they? That doesn't make them okay.

ANN *(Becoming more upset.)* Howard, here you go again! Assuming too much!

HOWARD What?

ANN I know that you live next door, and that you see more than I do. But you still can't keep assuming so many negative things about Mrs. Allen.

HOWARD Have you spent more than twenty minutes alone with her?

ANN I'm her therapist. You know I have!

HOWARD Ugghhh!

ANN Sure, she has her problems. I know that. But she's going to make it. I've pored over her file. She's improved a lot.

HOWARD But hasn't her file has been, like, questionable for some time? By the last therapist?

ANN By some people, yes. But her file is fine. The facility went over it. Over and over.

HOWARD But I heard there were, you know, some dis-agreements and stuff.

ANN In mental health there are always disagreements. And discrepancies. It's just part of the game.

HOWARD Ehhh . . .

(Pause. He tears open a light-stick, snaps it out of aggravation. It bursts into light. ANN stares at him, deep in thought.)

ANN Goodness, Howard. I've only been in therapy for a few years. But I've seen a lot. I've made a lot of bad assumptions about different clients. Making judgments—

HOWARD Oh, come on!

ANN No, hear me out! I spent so much time doing all of that. And I've learned how detrimental it can be. I can't . . . judge people on their *file* alone, or by just talking to them only a few times. Everybody is different. *Everybody.* It's bad enough that so many therapists are so quick to have everyone committed.

HOWARD So you should just throw out all the information?? All the data you have on people with mental trouble?

ANN I'm not saying *that*! But people . . . well, people are *complicated.* People can change. And it's all about second chances, right? In therapy, there's something called the Adam theory.

HOWARD *(Dismissively.)* Here we go . . .

ANN No, seriously. *Second chances.* That's what Mrs. Allen needs. She's going to make it. She just needs some nurturing.

HOWARD *(Wearily)* Well . . .

ANN She'll have her check-ins. She'll have her medication. She's probably headed over to her sister's right now. Meredith is here, at home, where she belongs. I'll try to get her to come to those emotion-in-motion meetings. It'll be good for her and her mother. *(Pause. She takes a breath.)* Mrs. Allen is going to be all right.

HOWARD Hmmmpph.

ANN Okay?

HOWARD Okay. Whatever. You're the expert. If you're confident, I'm confident.

ANN *That's* what I want to hear!

HOWARD Mh-hmm. Well. Second chances, huh?

ANN Yep.

HOWARD I do tend to assume the worst. My mom is always telling me that I do. Mrs. Allen *does* have her sweet side.

ANN There you go!

HOWARD I'm just exhausted, I guess. My math mid-term was a killer. I don't know if I have any brain cells left. Plus, all the time that I've been over here.

ANN It's okay! Come on, let's enjoy our Halloween!

(The doorbell rings.)

HOWARD Well, I'm trying . . .

ANN There they are!

(She moves to door but he jumps up and cuts her off.)

HOWARD Hey, it's my turn, right?

ANN Well, be my guest! *(Hands him witch hat, which he promptly puts on.)*

HOWARD Thank you. I never do this at my own house so it's the least I can do here.

ANN That's right!

HOWARD *(Opens door, passes out candy.)* Happy Halloween! Wow. You guys look great! Okay, here you go. Plenty here! Hi there, Mrs. Hamilton, how are you? Everything good? That's great! Okay, bye.

(Enter MEREDITH. She walks in, groggy, and gets a glass of water. HOWARD closes door and puts down candy. He picks a few pieces out and begins to eat them until the end of the play.)

HOWARD Hey . . . what's that old song that our parents used to sing? *(Singing)* 'Trick or treat, smell my feet—'

HOWARD & ANN 'Give me something good to eat!!'

(They both laugh.)

HOWARD So corny.

ANN Hey Meredith. How was your nap?

MEREDITH Great. Wow, sorry about that. I really passed out. I didn't know you guys were here.

HOWARD Hope you don't mind. We just came over to check on you. We brought you some food.

MEREDITH Well. Thank you. Last night was nuts. All that running around.

HOWARD We got you cheese fries.

MEREDITH Oh, good. Thank you. *(Pause.)* Ann, I'm probably not going to go to that haunted house thing.

ANN No? Okay. That's fine.

MEREDITH There's been so much going on. I just want to relax.

HOWARD I hear ya.

MEREDITH I appreciate you two being here, and bringing me food. You guys didn't have to come over.

HOWARD Aw, come on. That's what neighbors are for.

MEREDITH Um. You guys . . . weren't just arguing about *me*, were you?

ANN Huh?

MEREDITH I thought I heard you guys talking about me. Or maybe about my mom.

HOWARD Well . . .

MEREDITH Well *what*?

HOWARD Sorry . . . um . . .

ANN Howard's trying to convince me that there's more to your mom's condition that people think.

MEREDITH What do you mean?

ANN He and I basically disagree. That's all. I told him that your mother is going to be fine. Sometimes Howard just gets paranoid.

HOWARD Hey!

MEREDITH Well. I know how Howard can be.

ANN He thinks that the bump on your head was foul play.

MEREDITH I told both of you how I got this. We were arguing and I bumped into the cabinet door. That's it.

ANN See, Howard? Now, let's drop all of this. Please!

HOWARD Sorry.

MEREDITH It's okay. It's fine. *(Beat.)* But since we're on the subject . . . *did* you guys hear anything about my mom?

ANN Yes. We just found out, while you were sleeping. Her release was cleared from the Day Health Center.

MEREDITH WHAT? *When??*

ANN A few hours ago.

MEREDITH Already?

HOWARD They said they really couldn't hold her for more than twenty-four hours.

MEREDITH It's supposed to be forty-eight hours!

ANN It is. But you remember the last two times they did that.

MEREDITH Ughhh. Yes.

ANN She threatened the lawsuit again. She insisted that she did nothing wrong.

MEREDITH But she spray-painted paint all across the front window of that bakery! And then drove recklessly all over town. I told them that!

ANN And they couldn't prove a thing. She denied every bit of it.

MEREDITH Oh my . . .

ANN And then she threatened a lawsuit over and over. *(Pause.)* So, yeah. Dr. Fishman cleared her release. She went over to your aunt's.

MEREDITH Well . . . *(Bristles.) Damn.* Who are people going to believe? A bunch of shrinks or someone who spends every day with her?

(Beat. They take a long, curious look at MEREDITH.)

HOWARD Meredith, hang on. We . . . thought that everything was getting better around here.

MEREDITH Well, I don't know. They *were.* I guess. But . . . lately, it's kind of been the last straw.

ANN The last straw?

MEREDITH Yeah. Our arguing . . . and some of the words she used with me. It was . . . *(Suddenly.)* I mean, did they really release her??

ANN Yes.

MEREDITH I don't believe it. They didn't even call me.

HOWARD They said they tried. Twice. I think your phone's turned off.

ANN Look, we know that she has had some issues. But with medication—

MEREDITH Medication?? Are you still on *that*??

(Pause. They look at her, stunned.)

ANN Meredith, wait. I thought that we agreed on this. On her file.

MEREDITH Ann, there are a lot of things that *file* doesn't tell you.

ANN But there are a lot of things that it *does. (Beat.)* And, look. There's something you might want to consider.

MEREDITH What?

ANN You might want to consider . . . coming to my emotion-in-motion meetings. They're good for families that go through this kind of thing.

MEREDITH I can't believe what I'm hearing! I didn't report half of the things that happened in this house! Do you know that??

ANN Few families going through this kind of mental stress do. But I'd like for you to—

MEREDITH My God! Are you listening to yourself? NO! I'm not going to, to some *meeting.* To *therapy!! (Points to forehead.)* And no, I didn't get *this* from accidentally falling down.

HOWARD What??

MEREDITH You heard me.

ANN You're under duress. This is common.

MEREDITH And *you* don't live here!! You've only been her therapist for less than a year. And does that file really tell you what my mother has done?

HOWARD Meredith, take a breath. Come on. Relax.

MEREDITH No! This is it! I'm done protecting her. They should have never released her! *(Pause. She paces, in deep reluctance and agitation.)* I never wanted her to go to jail. Or anything like that.

ANN Nobody does!

MEREDITH But does that file tell you she once tried to poison me???

> *(Long pause as they stare at her in complete shock.)*

MEREDITH Does it say that she doesn't like children?

HOWARD Are you telling us . . . that she seriously tried to poison you?

MEREDITH I love my mother with all my heart. I *do*. But I just can't protect here anymore! I . . . *yes!* She tried to poison me! There. Now, everybody knows!

ANN Meredith, take it easy. You should seriously consider coming to these meetings.

MEREDITH SHE TRIED TO HARM MY FATHER!!
SHE TRIED TO POISON *HIM* TOO!!

(Long pause. They are in absolute shock.)

MEREDITH Why do you think he moved so far away? Is
that enough for you, Ann? You guys don't have ANY
IDEA!! I'M DONE TRYING TO HIDE THIS STUFF!!

HOWARD Your . . . your *father*?

*(MEREDITH bumps her foot into the bag of
candy. Beat.)*

MEREDITH Huh? What is this?? This isn't the candy that
I put out for Halloween!

HOWARD I got that bag from the garage, out by your
dryer. Sorry. It had the better candy in it. You know, for the
kids.

MEREDITH WHAT??

ANN Sorry, we should have asked you.

MEREDITH This bag was my mother's candy!! I threw it
out in the garage on purpose! To get it out of the way! *(She
snatches the candy bar from HOWARD's hands)* What have
you done??

ANN Oh . . .

MEREDITH You ate this . . .?

(Pause as HOWARD looks weakly at her and nods. He slowly grabs his chest.)

MEREDITH You . . . ATE THIS?

(Doorbell rings. The three of them are in total shock. They stare at the door. Lights fade to black. End of play.)

About the playwright

John Glass is a playwright and short story writer that lives in southern California. His plays have been produced in California, Michigan, Alabama, Texas and New York City. In 2013 John co-founded *Student Plays*, which specializes in scripts framed around Latino themes, American history, and also "spooky" themes. *Student Plays* also carries a number of adult plays, suitable for community and professional theater.

Contact John at john@studentplays.org

☞ More from Student Plays ☜

Othello's Just Another Fellow

Dramedy. **Grades 5-7.** 25-35 minutes. 8 actors: 4 males, 3 females, one teacher (or student portraying a teacher) 3 to 5 extras, if needed. ****A Latino-themed play****

A group of students are involved in a school production of *Othello*, but one of them is disturbed about the lack of diversity in the play. He takes certain steps to disrupt the play but in the end is encouraged by the others to try and make a difference in another, more constructive way. A lesson is learned, and the production is saved from disaster!

Pagasqueeny's Pantry

Comedy. **Middle/High School.** 15-20 minutes. 6 actors: 3 females, 2 males. One student (or a teacher) plays the comical role of the elderly Mr. Pagasqueeny.

Three friends sneak into Mr. Pagasqueeny's home to get something that one of them left behind. But in walks Pagasqueeny and they must hide in the pantry! In this comical play, a lesson is learned about honesty and trust, but it takes a heated discussion in the pantry and a subsequent attempt to escape to find this out!

Una Carta de Abuelo

Dramedy. **Middle/High School.** 35-45 minutes. 10 actors: 1 teacher, 5 females, 4 males. (With the option of 4-5 extra actors in two scenes.)   ****A Latino-themed play****

Two Latino cousins discover an old letter in their late grandfather's comic collection that they think leads to treasure! The cousins often butt heads, with one believing that he is more "Mexican," the other believing that some people make too much of a fuss about "being Mexican." Thus, they form their *own* groups in search of what Grandpa hid long ago. But what they find is actually worth more than merely silver or gold.

Barbecue at the Prom!

Dramedy. **Grades 5-8.** 25-35 minutes. 6 actors: 3 females, 3 males

It's a classic tale of guys versus girls! It's a prom committee, and everybody is supposed to work together but differences and opinions get in the way, causing the guys and girls to form their groups. For the end-of-the-year prom, one side wants pasta and lace, the other wants sports and barbecue! The two groups square off but eventually work together, demonstrating the importance of cooperation and compromise.

Going to Guatemala

Dramedy. **High School.** 50-60 minutes. 11 actors. 6 males, 5 females.   ****A Latino-themed play****

A Latino student is chosen at the last minute to join a humanitarian group from his school that is headed to Guatemala. But since his Spanish is weak, he faces ridicule and criticism from certain peers. Jealousy and anger trickle throughout the campus as the trip approaches, and the social buzz of the high school becomes even more hectic when the student's trip money is stolen on campus, jeopardizing his trip.

Stravinsky's Kitchen

Comedy. **High School/College.** 12-15 minutes. 3 actors: 3 males (or females).

Two friends secretly enter the home of an employer to obtain a forgotten object but the homeowner abruptly arrives home while they are there. As they hide in the kitchen's pantry and plot their getaway, the two talk and eventually argue, exposing the true colors of one of them. Upon their hasty exit a mistake is made, and one of them capitalizes on this mistake, resulting in his/her fortune.

Forty Whacks

Drama. Spooky. **High School/College.** 25-35 minutes. 3 actors: 2 females, 1 male.

A pair of siblings have inherited the Lizzie Borden Bed and Breakfast in New England. Although the business was run for decades in a quiet, respectable fashion, one of the siblings is over-ambitious, wanting to unearth an alleged piece of buried evidence within the house. This brings about a chilly tension between brother and sister, and perhaps within the house itself.

John Calhoun and a Thief

Drama. **College.** 35-40 minutes. 3 actors: 2 females, 1 male.

Kicked out of a university PhD program, a bitter and dejected female lifts from the library archives original copies of John Calhoun's personal documents. Counseled and consoled by her roommates, her conscience slowly gets to her; but as she seeks entry to other universities her luck turns to worse, and the subsequent decisions she makes regarding the historic papers cause this one-act play to become darker, if not funnier.

Honoring the Hijacker

Drama. **College.** 12-15 minutes. 4 actors: 2 females, 2 males.

It's 1981, the ten-year anniversary of the famed hijacker D.B. Cooper. The play's four characters are attending a "D.B. Festival" and have stayed up very late, outlasting everybody else. The late night chit-chat goes from pranks and jokes to outright volatility, and suddenly this get-together becomes something that three of the four characters didn't bargain for.

It's a Super Day at Sammy's!

Comedy. **Middle or High School.** 35-40 minutes. 9 actors: 5 females, 4 males (4 possible adults).

Jodi has found a summer job at a travel agency. But her three younger siblings can't seem to live without her! They call her at the office incessantly, which interferes with the work. The standard telephone greeting "It's a super day at Sammy's!" becomes a repeated theme of this comedy, as Jodi struggles to reach a balance between her job and her nagging siblings

Three Tenners

Comedy/Drama. **Elementary through High School.** Three Ten-Minute Plays.

Three Creepy Plays

Drama. **Middle School through College.** Three short 'creepy' plays.

Hockey Masks in Hueytown

Drama. Spooky. **High School/College.** 20-25 minutes. 4 actors: 2 males, 2 females.

Driving home for Thanksgiving break, four college students stop off in a small rural town to retrieve one of the student's old family pictures. They reluctantly enter the empty home of his deceased uncle, a former producer for the Friday the 13th movies. Strange objects are found during their search . .   but when a hockey mask surfaces, everything really goes sideways.

The Witch Makes Five

Drama. Spooky. **High School.** 10 minutes. 4 actors: 2 males, 2 females.

After a bizarre group camping trip, a student is checked into a youth mental facility . When she is visited by the other members of the trip, memories of the weekend trickle out . . . and horrific things begin to happen.

Mrs. Calapooza and the Culebra

Dramedy. **Grades 5-8.** 10 minutes. 5 actors: 3 females, 2 males.

Fed up with their grouchy teacher's classroom ways, four students complain and bicker back and forth during a Spanish quiz. The situation grows worse when the friends discover that one of them has pulled the ultimate prank on the teacher.

Raiders of the Lost Rakasa

Dramedy. **Grades 5-8.** 10 minutes. 7 actors: 4 females, 3 males.

Seven young explorers arrive at a cave in a far-off land in search of the great "Rakasa." They find what they want . . . along with a few of the cave's unexpected surprises.

Made in the USA
Monee, IL
07 July 2026

56550204R00036